This book
belongs to

....

To dearest Kay, with love

FREDERICK WARNE

Published by the Penguin Group
Penguin Books Ltd, 80 Strand, London WC2R 0RL, England
Penguin Young Readers Group, 345 Hudson Street,
New York, New York 10014, U.S.A.
Penguin Books Australia Ltd, 250 Camberwell Road, Camberwell,
Victoria 3124, Australia
Canada, India, New Zealand, South Africa

1 3 5 7 9 10 8 6 4 2

ISBN-13: 978 072326286 2

Printed in Great Britain

Lily's Seaside Adventure

by Pippa Le Quesne

Welcome to the Flower Fairies' Garden!

Where are the fairies?
Where can we find them?
We've seen the fairy-rings
They leave behind them!

Is it a secret
No one is telling?
Why, in your garden
Surely they're dwelling!

No need for journeying,
Seeking afar:
Where there are flowers,
There fairies are!

Contents

Pffffff. The little Flower Fairy stuck out her bottom lip and tried blowing her bangs off her face, but the mere effort was exhausting.

Wearily, she clambered to her feet and squinted across the lawn to see what her friends in the opposite flowerbed were up to. Her usually flowing white dress clung to the backs of her legs and her pearly wings drooped like two limp petals. Lily-of-the-Valley couldn't remember such a hot summer. Even on

1

the shady side of the garden, where
her flowers grew, it was stifling. Normally,
she was bursting with energy, but the
relentless heat of the last week had left
her wilting like a parched plant.

The Flower Fairy shuddered at the
thought of the lovely garden becoming
dried out and dying. Thank goodness the
kind humans who owned the house at the
top of the lawn never forgot their watering
duties. Without their help, the Flower
Fairies' Garden would be in real trouble.
Not only did the evening shower revive

all the flowers and keep the grass from browning, but it was the highlight of the fairies' day too. Being careful to keep out of sight of the humans, they would stand under the dripping leaves of their plants and enjoy a deliciously cool soaking. And then, for a few hours, the refreshed garden would come to life and be full of its usual activity and happy chatter.

Lily mopped her brow with her petal handkerchief and studied the pansies over in the rockery. There was no sign of movement now.

It had been such a muggy night that sleep had
been impossible, and she guessed that most
of her friends were napping in the shade.
In fact, she could just make out a leg dangling
over the side of the leaf hammock that hung
between two stems. Despite the shoe having
been kicked off, she recognized Dandelion's
bright yellow stocking. She groaned.
Not even Dandelion, who could barely
sit still for a second, had any energy today.

Lily, too, had spent much of the morning
trying to sleep, but had managed no more
than a light doze. And now she was bored
with trying and in need of a distraction.

"Right," she decided out loud, "I'm off to find some company. And I know just the fairy. Willow has water *and* shade, so she *must* be awake."

* * *

"Ahhhhhhhhh." Lily let out a long sigh, as she swirled her feet around in the pool under the weeping willow tree. That was more like it. After the exertion of flying all the way to the bottom of the garden, the little Flower Fairy had practically collapsed in a heap on the grass. But making one last effort, she had wiggled over to the edge of the pond and splashed her face with huge handfuls

of water. It restored her immediately and
now she was sitting on the bank, happily
watching a family of dragonflies darting
between the willow leaves, their
bodies flashing brilliant
blue in the glinting sunlight. They
appeared to be playing-hide and-seek, and it
looked like fun.

Surprisingly, there was no sign of Willow.
Lily had peered up into the mass of long
bending branches and called out her
friend's name, but there had been
no reply.

Perhaps she's gone diving, Lily
thought to herself. *And who can
blame her?* She gazed at the deep
pool, thinking how lucky her
friend was to have the
special gift of
being able

to breathe underwater and swim with the fish. She wished she could go in just for a quick dip. But the little Flower Fairy knew that no matter how tempting it looked, water could be incredibly dangerous if you couldn't swim or weren't a strong swimmer. *Hmm.* What was the next best thing on a stifling hot day? *Oooh—a nice breeze*, Lily decided, letting her mind wander to all the big open spaces that she could think of ... There was the marsh, and the meadow ...

The meadow! That was it. There was sure to be a light wind over the sloping field. And it was just a short distance down the lane. "Now, why didn't I think of that sooner?" Lily exclaimed, suddenly feeling more energetic than she had in days. She stooped to dip her handkerchief in the pool and tied it dripping wet around her neck. It would keep her nicely cool on the journey.

Then picking up her Lily-of-the-Valley staff, she set off towards the stone wall that divided the garden from the outside world. Her snowy white flowers were arranged on a long slender stem and they nodded and tinkled as she walked, alerting the other Flower Fairies to her presence. Lily took it everywhere.

This is going to be great, she thought to herself. A trip to the meadow was just the change of scene that she needed and, best of all, it was home to two of her dearest friends—Buttercup and Cowslip.

Chapter Two
Midsummer Madness

The three Flower Fairies sat side by side in the shady nook of an oak, gazing out across the meadow and sipping fennel tea.

Lily was delighted to see her friends, but she had been wrong about the breeze. Not a leaf or even a blade of grass stirred, and she was *so* disappointed. If at all possible, it felt even hotter and drier out here.

"Oh, Lily, you are funny."
Cowslip chuckled, gathering up
her wavy brown hair and twisting
it in a knot on top of her head.
"There are no watering cans,
sprinklers, or hoses in the wild.
The only water we've seen for the
last week has been the dew. And thank
goodness that's been kind enough to keep
appearing each morning!"

"I just didn't think it through," Lily
replied, remembering now just *how* still it
had been in the garden. "It's so sheltered
where I live that it's hard to tell if there's
any wind beyond the walls."

"Never mind. It's a real treat to see you,
anyway," Buttercup said kindly. "But
we're just the same. This heat is driving
us crazy!" Lily smiled at her friend.
Her cheeks were bright pink and she looked

uncomfortably hot, but she was still her
usual cheerful self.

After exchanging gossip and catching up
on each other's news, the three of them fell
into an easy silence. The view from the oak
tree was fantastic. A carpet of patchwork
fields spread out before them, dotted with
wild flowers and marked out by hedgerows.

Flower Fairies lived all around, but there was very little movement apart from some cows lazily grazing and a tractor rolling along the country lanes. Everyone seemed to be feeling sluggish apart from the birds, who continued to chirp joyfully. A graceful pair of swallows swooped low over the meadow, occasionally diving for an insect, before soaring high into the sky to hover on the warm air currents.

"If I were a bird," mused Cowslip, breaking the silence, "I wouldn't waste any time inland today. I'd go straight to the

coast and enjoy
the lovely sea breeze."

"Oh yes," piped up Buttercup.
"Not that we've ever been there. But the gulls
come and visit us sometimes, and they're
incredibly chatty—full of stories about the
beach and how much fun the sea is and how
it's the *only* place to be during the summer."

"So I've heard," said Lily enthusiastically.
"I met Sea-Pink and Horned Poppy at the
Spring Ball and they told me all about
their beach life.
It sounded so
exciting..." She
drained her tea and
absentmindedly
placed the empty
acorn cup in
her lap. "You
know... I

did promise them a visit—"

Buttercup and Cowslip looked at her as she stopped mid-sentence and furrowed her brow in thought. All of a sudden, she leaped to her feet, sending the acorn shell clattering down the tree trunk. "Oops!" Lily giggled then turned to her friends. "Listen, what better time is there to visit the seaside than when it's too hot to be anywhere else?" she burst out, her eyes shining with eagerness. "Imagine paddling in the rock pools and feeling cool sand between your toes? Come on! What are we waiting for?"

"Er, um," mumbled Cowslip, thinking it through. "It's a wonderful idea. But it's such a long way."

"I'd love to go,' Buttercup agreed, "but we'd never make it there and back in a day."

"Well, no . . . But," Lily went on, "if you think about it, it's only just past the marsh. So we could stop there for tonight and then first thing tomorrow we'd be by the sea. We wouldn't be away for that long . . . Oh, go on," she pleaded. "It'd be such an adventure—a night under the stars and then a morning of fun at the beach!"

Her friends looked at one another then nodded their consent. "OK," Cowslip said, her face breaking into a grin. "You're on!"

"We've nearly made it!" Lily announced brightly, spotting a patch of purple mallow a stone's throw away. She flew back to the ground to join her friends.

It had been a long, hot journey from the meadow to the marsh, and the three Flower Fairies were feeling thirsty and dishevelled. They'd hoped to come across a friendly bird that might give them a lift, but they weren't in luck and, with no time to waste, they had persevered on foot and on wing.

Lily was so excited about their excursion that she'd forgotten her tiredness, but glancing at the other two it was obvious that their spirits were fading. So after suggesting they take a break, she'd launched herself into the air to try to work out their exact whereabouts. The ground had become spongy underfoot and for a while now they'd been pushing their way through long grass, so they knew they'd reached the marsh, but they were looking specifically for Mallow—one of the wild fairies known for her hospitality. Naughty elves lived in the area too and, although they didn't mean the Flower Fairies any real harm, they were experts at making a nuisance of themselves and playing tricks on unsuspecting travelers. So it was best to stay close to a fairy who called the marsh home and knew every elf prank in the book.

"Thank goodness," said Cowslip, getting to her feet. "I wasn't sure that I could take another step, but if it's not much further . . ."

"And it'll be good to see Mallow," added Buttercup, visibly perkier since Lily had broken the good news. "But what happens if she's not—"

"There?" said a voice, and from out of a nearby clump of rush-grass stepped a tall, slightly scruffy fairy, with dark hair in two long plaits and a very pretty face.

"Mallow!" exclaimed Lily, rushing to hug her. "How did you find us?"

"Who can mistake the tinkling of Lily-of-the-Valley's bells?" said the older fairy with a twinkle in her eye.

"I hadn't thought of that," replied Lily, putting down her staff. She was so used to their gentle ringing that she didn't really notice it anymore. "We're lucky that it didn't attract the elves, aren't we?" she added, feeling slightly concerned for their safety.

"You don't need to worry about the elves," Mallow said reassuringly. "They're troublesome but completely harmless. But what are you doing in these parts, anyway? It's not often we have the pleasure of a visit from a Garden Fairy."

"We're on our way to the seaside!" exclaimed Lily, feeling rather proud of their daring plan.

"What a good idea!" The Marsh Fairy nodded her approval. "Now—who's hungry and who needs a drink?"

"Oh, yes please," chorused Buttercup and Cowslip without hesitation.

"I thought so," Mallow replied merrily, unpacking a knapsack that she'd set on the ground. "I always carry plenty of provisions—so we can camp here tonight. As long I've

got the stars as a canopy, I'll sleep anywhere!"

Within minutes, Mallow's visitors were happily munching on her special fairy cheeses and washing them down with dandelion and burdock juice. And when they had finished their picnic, they were surprised to find that not only did they feel satisfied but somehow stronger as well—as though there was an element of fairy magic thrown

in with the ingredients. Lily stretched and yawned. She felt quite content.

Dusk was approaching and it was still very warm, but the dampness of the marsh made for a pleasant atmosphere, and the prospect of lying under a blanket of twinkling stars sounded very inviting. After Mallow's reassuring words about the elves she felt sure that they'd all sleep well tonight—and the next morning they'd wake to the prospect of their very own seaside expedition!

Chapter Three
Unfamiliar Territory

Wooo. Woo, woo, wooooo.

Lily snapped awake.

Expecting to see the familiar shapes of the garden, she was disorientated by the towering grass and big open sky. *Where was she?*

Woooo. Wooo-wooo.

"Who's there?" The little fairy sat up and looked around, her heart pounding in her chest.

Then she spotted the slumbering forms of her three friends and remembered they were camping out on the marsh. *OK*, she thought to herself. *Calm down—it's just new surroundings to get used to. You're perfectly safe.*

But what was that spooky wailing?

Getting to her feet and taking a deep breath, she decided to investigate. There was no point in waking the others until she knew what they were dealing with. So, stepping carefully over Cowslip, she cupped a hand  behind her ear and listened intently. The wailing seemed to have stopped. The marsh was completely still now, and the only sound she could hear was the gentle breathing of her companions. *Silly me*, Lily told herself. *Must have been a barn owl.*

However, she was just about to settle herself back down when there was a rustling noise behind her. She spun round just in time

to see the rush-grass parting . . . And from
out of it floated . . . a ghostly green face!
"AGGGGGGGHHHHH!" screamed

Lily, stumbling backwards and tripping
over Cowslip, who shrieked in surprise.
The two Flower Fairies clung to one another,
trembling with fear

"What's going on?" Mallow's calm voice
cut through the chaos.

"I heard a noise . . . And . . . and . . .
then this face came out of the darkness . . .
Oh, it was terrible . . ." Lily whimpered her
explanation. Although the illuminated face

had disappeared, she was still shaking. And Buttercup, who was awake and frightened too, was sobbing with relief at the sight of the bold Marsh Fairy.

Just then there was the sound of muffled giggling.

"Aha! It's those elves," Mallow said immediately. "Amusing themselves by scaring you with their ghost trick."

The giggling stopped immediately.

"But how?" asked Lily, instantly comforted by the possibility of a straightforward explanation. She was a courageous fairy at heart. Besides, the soft light of dawn had begun to dilute the inky blackness and it was easier to feel brave in the daytime.

"I'll show you," Mallow replied. "ELVES!" she boomed. "Come out here, RIGHT AWAY!"

There was some urgent whispering and then from out of the rush-grass appeared a couple of shame-faced elves.

"Well," said Mallow. "What have you got to say for yourselves?"

"Um, sorry?" muttered one of the elves. The answer was barely audible.

The Marsh Fairy raised an eyebrow and then turned her attention on the speaker's friend, who was trying to suppress a smirk. "And you?"

"Sorry," he mumbled reluctantly. "But you've got to admit it was a pretty good joke."

"Ahem," said the other elf, clearing his throat. "We did it like this." And he lifted his cupped hands up to his friend's face and opened them. There, sitting between his palms was a sleepy glow-worm, giving off a strong green light that lit up the other elf's face.

"Oh, I get it!" announced Buttercup. "You were both entirely hidden in the dark other than *your* face that had the light shining on it. So—"

"It looked like it was floating!" Cowslip finished her sentence.

Lily grinned with relief and then the corners of her mouth twitched and she began to giggle. "Oooh, I nearly jumped out of my skin," she spluttered, suddenly seeing the funny side of it.

The elves stared at her in surprise. They were used to being told off for their antics. Then one of them slapped her on the back and danced on the spot with glee.

"Woo, woo, wooooo!" howled his companion before bursting into laughter.

Suddenly Mallow began to chuckle too, and it was so infectious that soon all four Flower Fairies and the two mischievous elves were rolling around with laughter. And as the sun rose over the marsh, all ill-will was forgotten and the incident had turned into a jolly good joke.

After a hearty breakfast shared with the elves, the three Flower Fairies had set off immediately, in order to make the most of their day. Mallow bade them a fond farewell and pointed them in the right direction. "Follow your noses," she had said mysteriously. And sure enough, it was not long before the air had an unfamiliar tang to it . . .

And soon after that, they felt the first whisperings of a longed-for breeze. There was no mistaking it—it was the salty seaside air!

Now, Lily was standing next to Cowslip on a hillock, her arm resting on her friend's shoulder. Just below them, a pebbled slope gave way to an inviting shoreline of pale yellow sand and clear blue sea, stretching off into the distance.

Buttercup was sitting on the grass beside them, occupied with the business of pulling off her shoes and tugging at her leaf-green stockings. There was not a cloud in the sky and the temperature was already rising.

All of a sudden, Lily threw her staff to the ground and hitched up her long white gown. "Come on, you two!" she yelled. She was impatient to feel the silky sand beneath her feet and the cold water rushing over her toes. "Race you down there." And much to her friends' amusement, she began scrambling down the stony bank as if her life depended on it.

Chapter Four
A Whole New World

"Ta-da!" said Lily as she pressed a fan-shaped shell into the top of her castle. She'd dug a mound of sand and then carefully patted it into shape before decorating it with seaweed. She was having *so* much fun.

Buttercup and Cowslip had raced down to the sea after her and soon the three of them were skipping about in the foamy white water that foamed on to the beach. Then, when they had worn themselves out from running and splashing and laughing until their sides ached, they'd collapsed on the ground to dry off. And it wasn't long before they'd found a new activity and soon they were happily absorbed, playing in the sand.

Cowslip was busy burying her feet, having discovered how nice and cool it kept them, and Buttercup was scooping up handfuls of

soggy sand from the bottom of a rock pool. By dripping it slowly from her clenched fist, it created peaks and pinnacles that looked like towers. They were having a brilliant time.

"I could really do with a drink," Lily announced, now that she'd completed her masterpiece. The sun was rising higher in the sky and the refreshing effect of their dip in the water had quickly worn off. "And we could probably do with spending a bit of time in the shade."

"Yes, you're right," Cowslip agreed, leaning back on her hands and pulling her feet out of their sandy cocoon.

"I could stay here forever." Buttercup sighed with contentment. "But a drink would be good."

"Well, let's go and sit up there," Lily said, pointing to a plant at the top of the shingle with large crinkly ash-colored leaves. It looked like an invitingly shady spot. "Hang on a minute—aren't those yellow flowers horned poppies?"

There had been no sign as yet of Sea-Pink or Horned Poppy and despite enjoying themselves tremendously, Lily felt it would be a shame not to bump into their seaside friends.

"Let's go and look, shall we?" replied Cowslip, standing up and offering Buttercup a helping hand.

"Finding our friends would make today just perfect!" proclaimed Buttercup as the three fairies flew slowly up the steep slope.

"Hmm, I couldn't agree more," said Lily, suddenly feeling that their time was going all too quickly. She wasn't ready to consider their return journey quite yet. They'd only got to know one bit of the beach so far, and she'd spotted an interesting-looking island that she wouldn't mind exploring. *If only we could spend tomorrow here too,* the Garden Fairy thought to herself. If they hadn't been in the middle of such a hot spell then it wouldn't have been a problem, but a Flower Fairy's priority was always their plant and it was a responsibility they took very seriously, particularly in extreme weather conditions. Lily was just wondering if her flowers were faring well without their usual daily attention and hoping the humans hadn't gone on vacation, when a male voice broke into her thoughts.

"Ahoy there, land fairies! What brings you to these parts?" And from out between the leaves of the golden-flowered plant, appeared the merry face of Horned Poppy.

* * *

"So what is *that*?" asked Lily, once they'd
exchanged greetings with their new friend
and told him about their expedition. She
was pointing to the rocky outcrop that had
caught her interest earlier. It was a little
island topped with waving flower spikes
and connected to the beach by a narrow
sand causeway. It looked *fascinating*.

" Oh, nothing really," replied
Horned Poppy casually, "just a land mass.

But *I* use it as a lookout post."

"How exciting to have a lookout post!" Buttercup gasped. "And out at sea, as well."

"Well, it's no different to you climbing a tree in the meadow to find out what's going on," Horned Poppy commented. "But, yes, as far as I'm concerned, it's pretty special."

Lily grinned at him. He was such good company and so enthusiastic. Even the auburn curls that poked out of his green hood bounced around as he spoke. She imagined that every day was an adventure to him.

"Ooh, can we visit it?" implored Cowslip. "And meet the fairy who lives there?"

"Well," answered Horned Poppy, "even

though sea plantain does grow there, it isn't a Flower Fairy's home. Perhaps there's one living in another crop further down the coast, although I've never met her. But of course we can go and explore! Only, it would have to be tomorrow," he explained. Then in response to the confused expression on Lily's face, he continued, "The tide is rising, and although there'd be time to get out to the island, we'd be cut off from the beach within the hour. So it's just too risky."

Cowslip and Buttercup looked disappointed, but they knew they couldn't prolong their trip. Like Lily, they knew that in such stifling heat it would be unwise to leave their plants unattended for much longer.

It was Cowslip that spoke for them all. "As much as we'd love to stay, I'm afraid it's impossible. We really have to get home tonight, so we've got a lot of ground to cover this afternoon."

Horned Poppy nodded in response. "Well, you'll just have to come back another time!" he said brightly. "Now, we must go and visit Sea-Pink. She'd never forgive me if she knew that you'd come all this way and not dropped in on her. And you must be ready for some lunch by now?"

"Oh yes," Buttercup answered eagerly, "I'm starving."

"Me too," said Lily. Then, remembering her manners, she added, "That would be lovely, thank you."

"That's settled, then," said Horned Poppy. "And after lunch we'll see if we can find a gull to speed you home. Don't worry about your flowers—they'll be just fine. They're always much more resilient than we think. Now, follow me, we've got a bit of a climb ahead of us. Great views from Sea-Pink's home, though." And with that, the jovial fellow began skipping along a path that wound around the headland, continuing his happy commentary as he went.

Chapter Five
A Hasty Decision

They hadn't been going for more than a few
minutes when Lily realized she'd forgotten
something. "Oh bother," she said out loud.
"I've left my staff behind. Listen, I'll fly back
and catch up with you in no time. There's a
path all the way, right?"

"Yup," Horned Poppy replied. "Just keep
following it. And you can't miss Sea-Pink's
flowers. There are lots of them, and they're
like bright pink ornaments."

"OK," Lily called over her shoulder,
taking to the air to retrace
their steps.

She flitted back
quickly the way that
they'd come and in a

matter of moments, she spotted her beloved flowers, snowy white against the purple and brown pebbles that bordered Horned Poppy's patch.

"There you are," she murmured, giving them a jiggle so that they rang reassuringly. She was just about to set off again when the little island caught her eye once more. *It looks so magical*, she thought to herself. *If I was fast, I could run along the causeway, take a quick look and then fly back and find the others.* Lily thought for a moment.

There was something about the island that enchanted her. She remembered what Horned Poppy had said about the tide, but surely time was still on her side? It would be a mad dash and pretty exhausting, but it had to be worth it!

* * *

Lily sunk into the carpet of sea plantain. She felt truly humbled. Although she was constantly amazed by all the beautiful and incredible things that were a part of nature, she had never come across anything as magnificent as the sea before.

The island was still connected to the beach by the narrow walkway, but looking out towards the horizon, Lily felt as if she was entirely surrounded by the deep and mysterious water. It was very big and completely unfamiliar, *but not in a bad way*, Lily decided.

There was something calming about the sound of the waves lapping against the rock and without being aware of it happening, the little Garden Fairy became quite hypnotized and totally unaware of the passage of time.

* * *

"Oh no!"

Lily scrambled to her feet. It was the second time in the last twenty-four hours that she had woken with a jolt. This time she was shocked to realize that she had nodded off out at sea, curled up in the sea plantain.

And taking a hasty look around, she realized with a sinking heart that she really was *out at sea*. For, just as Horned Poppy had warned her, the tide had come in, and the small island was now cut off entirely from the beach.

In fact, *where was the beach?* Lily's immediate surroundings were clearly visible—the bendy sea plantain stems with their yellow and mauve flower spikes and the rocks where they met the sea—but looking towards the beach, all she could see was a wall of white. What was going on?

"Maybe I've just got disorientated and I'm facing the wrong direction and that's just the horizon that I'm looking at . . ." Lily said out loud as she began to walk around the outside edge of the island, feeling sure she'd catch sight of the sandy shore at any second. But she was in no such luck. The sea was on every side and further than that there was nothing, except . . .

Oh gosh, Lily gulped as her situation dawned on her. She was stuck on an island and

surrounded entirely by ... white ...
swirling ... mist.

"How did that happen? How could I have
been so foolish?" the little fairy scolded
herself. "And what am I going to do now?"
Her bottom lip trembled. She felt more
isolated than she could ever remember.
Being a garden Flower Fairy meant that even
at times when she chose her own company
and retreated to a quiet spot, she still knew
her friends were close by. Not only was she
completely alone now, but she also couldn't
even begin to guess in which *direction* her
friends were to be found. A fat tear slid

down her cheek and then another and
another. Before she knew it, she was
bawling her eyes out.

When she had got it out of her system
and there were no more tears left, Lily
stopped crying. And although nothing
had changed, she found that she didn't
feel quite so desperate.

"Right," she said, trying to make her voice
sound brave. "Now that I've felt sorry for
myself, I should probably try and work
out what to do." She picked up her staff and
took some comfort from the reassuring
feel of the stem in her hand. "So, as I
can't walk or swim back to land, that
just leaves flight ... but then I can't
see where I'm going and I could easily
wear myself out by flying in the wrong
direction and I might not be able to find
the island again ..."

As she worked through her options she passed the staff from one hand to another, glad to have it with her and to hear the soft ringing of its bells. The heavy mist had laid a cloak over the sea and it seemed to have gone to sleep, for there was an unearthly silence all around her.

"I guess I could wait here until the mist clears." Lily continued to ponder the problem. "But presumably a cold front must be coming for there to be mist in the first place and who knows how long it will last . . ." The little Flower Fairy shivered at the thought of a night out at sea with no real cover, nothing to drink and no food. She put down her staff and dug her hands into her deep pockets, hoping that there might be a forgotten nut or dried berry that she could nibble on.

There was no food of any description but as her fingers closed around a small package her heart leaped. *Could it be?*

Lily pulled out the neatly folded sycamore leaf and laying it on her the ground, carefully opened it up.

"Oh, thank goodness!" She let out a huge sigh of relief and a surge of hope rushed through her. For there, lying in a small heap, was a gleaming pile of fairy dust.

Chapter Six
A Lesson Learned

"Fairy dust, fairy dust, lend me a hand, and carry the sound of my bells to the land!"

Lily-of-the-Valley released the handful of pollen particles and watched them tumble down the length of her staff, which she'd wedged in a crack in the rock. As there was no wind to carry it off, the dust coated the petals of each and every flower as it fell. *So far, so good,* Lily thought nervously, as she shut her eyes and willed the magic to work.

Flower Fairies aren't able to cast powerful spells, but by harvesting the pollen from their plants and grinding it up they can create fairy dust. And, in times of need, this precious powder enables them to conjure up their own special bit of magic. As far as Lily knew it had never failed before, but she also knew that there was always a first for everything. She crossed her fingers tightly.

Ding dong, ding dong.

The Garden Fairy nearly jumped out of her skin. What on earth was that? Her eyes flew open.

Ding. Dinnnngggg. DING.

"Well, I never!" the little Flower Fairy exclaimed, for it was coming from her staff. It was very odd to hear her delicate flowers making so much noise and she couldn't quite believe her ears. The staff looked completely normal—despite the fact that the bells were swinging back and forth without her shaking them—but the sound that was coming from them was unrecognizable. It was so loud and clear that it could only be described as the chiming of church bells.

Lily stood in the middle of the sea plantain, hugging herself with her arms. The only thing the little Flower Fairy could do now was to hope and wait. The mist had turned into an enveloping fog, and the air was growing chillier with every passing moment.

And for the first time in as long as she could remember, she actually felt cold—and it wasn't half as nice as she'd expected.

"The fairy dust will wear off soon," Lily said out loud, realizing that when it did, the ringing of her flowers would be reduced to nothing more than a tinkle. She swallowed hard and tried not to think about it. She'd used up all her fairy dust in one go, so it was crucial that her friends heard the ringing and came to find her. She closed her eyes tightly and wished as hard as she could. *Please come and rescue me. Someone.*

* * *

"Lily!"

The Garden Fairy gasped. It was ever so faint, but she was certain she had just heard her name being called. Not daring to move a muscle, she held her breath and listened.

"Lily!"

There it was, distinct and close by.

"YES—I'M HERE!" she shouted at the top of her voice, springing to her feet and rushing to the edge of the island. She strained her eyes to see through the blanket of fog, but it was too thick and there was no clue as to where the call had come from.

Suddenly there was a great rush of air and

from out of nowhere, just a wingspan away,
an enormous gull landed right in front of
her. And there, huddled on its back, were her
friends. They had come to rescue her!

"Oh, thank goodness! It really is
you." Cowslip reached her first and then
Buttercup, Horned Poppy, and Sea-Pink
were all hugging her at once. They began
bombarding her with questions and she
couldn't hear herself think, but the little
Flower Fairy didn't care. She was safe again,

and it was the best feeling in the world.

* * *

"And it can stay hot forever, as far as I'm concerned," Lily announced.

It was the following afternoon, and she was back in the garden regaling the tale of her sea rescue to Dandelion, Pansy, and Marigold. After a long night's sleep, which even the mugginess didn't disturb, Lily had spent the morning giving her plant her undivided attention. Now she was sharing a cup of tea with her neighbors.

"As long as I'm safely in the garden, I won't ever complain again," she finished, beaming at her audience.

"Wow! What an adventure you've had." Daring Dandelion looked a little envious. "A trip to the beach, being stranded out at sea, *and* a ride home on a gull's back."

"I had a fantastic time," Lily agreed, "but only until I got lost. That was scary and no fun at all. And I've definitely learned not to be so impetuous."

"Impet-you-what?" asked Marigold, twirling a strand of red hair in her fingers and looking confused.

"Impetuous," Lily replied, ruffling her younger friend's hair. It was good to be surrounded by familiar faces. She hadn't forgotten the awful feeling of loneliness she'd felt on her own in the middle of the sea. "It means making hasty decisions without thinking them through."

"Oh yes." Pansy nodded wisely and gave her a knowing look.

Lily felt herself reddening. She was known among her friends for being impulsive and she'd always thought it was a good thing. But she really had learned her lesson. Being spontaneous was good, but not listening to advice was just foolish. Luckily for her, Horned Poppy hadn't been at all cross that she'd ignored what he'd said about the tide; and Buttercup and Cowslip had been so relieved to see her that they hadn't scolded her either. But once they'd been dropped off in the meadow and she was alone on the back of the gull, Lily had taken the time to think. The whole fiasco had given her quite a fright and she'd come to the conclusion that she was very lucky that nothing more serious had happened. So she'd made a vow on her staff that she'd be much more careful in future and much less *impetuous*.

"Funny that it was misty and cold on the coast," commented Pansy, noticing her friend's embarrassment and changing the subject. "It's stayed just the same here. Absolutely scorching!"

"Apparently the weather's much more changeable by the sea," Dandelion chimed in.

Lily nodded in agreement. "That's what Sea-Pink told us." She paused for a second and then added,

"You know, the beach is a great place to visit, but next time I'll be more careful and listen to my friend Horned Poppy." And with that, the happy Garden Fairy patted her trusty staff and laid down on the ground beside it. She had decided—for the rest of the day all she was going to do was relax in the sunshine, take pleasure in the feel of the heat on her face, and enjoy every single minute of it.

FLOWER
FAIRIES™
FRIENDS

Visit our Flower Fairies website at:

www.flowerfairies.com

There are lots of fun Flower Fairy games and
activities for you to play, plus you can find out more
about all your favorite fairy friends!

Log onto the
Flower Fairies
Friendship Ring

Visit the Flower Fairies website to sign up for the new
Flower Fairies Friendship Ring!

★ No membership fee
★ News and updates
★ Every new friend receives a special gift!
(while supplies last)